Hidden Treasure

Parables for Kids

by Margaret N. Freeman

illustrated by John Ham

 ®
STANDARD PUBLISHING

Cincinnati, Ohio   2728

Library of Congress Cataloging in Publication Data

Freeman, Margaret N.
    Hidden treasure.

    Summary: A collection of short devotional stories,
each accompanied by a suggested Bible reading and
a prayer.
    1. Children—Prayer-books and devotions—English.
    1. Prayer books and devotions   I. Ham, John, ill.
    II. Title.
BV4870.F8   242'.62   81-16669
ISBN 0-87239-499-9   AACR2

To my treasured grandchildren
Erik,
Emily,
Lindsey,
and Michael

"The kingdom of heaven is like treasure hidden in a field. When a man found it, he hid it again, and then in his joy went and sold all he had and bought that field" (Matthew 13:44).

"I have hidden your word in my heart that I might not sin against you" (Psalm 119:11).

May this book help you to love your Bible more as you search for treasures daily.

How to Serve

"Serve one another in love" (Galatians 5:13).

Dan had been sick for a long time. He was almost well again, but he had become so accustomed to having people wait on him that he had become a bit lazy.

"Linda!" he yelled at his sister, "Go make me a sandwich. I'm hungry!"

Linda patiently laid aside the dustcloth she was using and started for the kitchen.

Then Dan realized how tired Linda looked. *She has*

been running dozens of errands for me every day for weeks, and she helps Mother a lot, too, he thought.

"Say, Linda," he said gently, "why don't you sit down and rest? Look at this new book of mine, and I'll make us both sandwiches."

Linda sank down into the chair and gave her brother a grateful smile.

Treasure Hunt: John 13:12-17

Let's think about this:
   What do we think it means to be great?
   How does that compare with Jesus' example?

A prayer: Father, forgive me for failing to serve in love so many times. Help me not to be selfish, but make me willing to do my best for You and others. Amen.

A song to sing: "When There's Love at Home"

Giants

"He rescued me from my powerful enemy" (Psalm 18:17).

So you think there aren't any giants any more?

David got the best-known one when he polished off nine-and-a-half-foot Goliath with his slingshot. David vanquished the giant because God was with him, and David, with his loyal heart, realized this.

This is also the way we can get rid of the "giants" in our lives, and we all face them every day—falsehood, anger, pride, selfishness, and other giant-sized temptations.

Judy, for instance, had money saved for the Sunday-school offering. But all the kids were buying double-dip ice cream cones. Ummm! they looked good! Judy rubbed her hot forehead and clutched the coins a little tighter. Did Judy have a giant to fight?

Dan wanted to join the boys in the park. They called as they ran past: "Bring your ball and glove and come on!" As Dan ran in to get his ball and glove, little brother Buddy whined and tugged at his mother's skirt. Mother looked tired as she tried to finish her canning. She looked hopefully at Dan as he came in. Did Dan have a giant to fight?

David, with God's help, won his battle with the giant Goliath. With God's help, we too will be able to conquer giants of temptation.

Treasure Hunt: 1 Samuel 17:38-51

Let's think about *our weaknesses:* Let's face the question squarely—What clutters up my life most that keeps me from being my best? Let's conquer *that* giant today—with God's help!

A prayer: Dear Lord, help me face the giants in my life honestly. Help me do as David did—rely on You for help, so that I can win my battle against sin and wrong. In Jesus' name I pray, amen.

A song to sing: "Onward, Christian Soldiers"

7

Caring Means Sharing

"Faith by itself, if it is not accompanied by action, is dead" (James 2:17).

Mrs. MacGregor lived in a large house on a hill. To the people living in the little shacks in the valley below, that house looked like a mansion. Mrs. MacGregor owned the mill where most of these people worked. She also owned the shabby shacks they lived in. She paid them the lowest wages it was possible to pay. But Mrs. MacGregor and her ten-year-old son Gene had everything money could buy.

"Gene, you and I must set a good example for these poor people who do not know right from wrong," Mrs. MacGregor would say. "We must give them a Christian example by being regularly in our places in church on Sunday morning." So they swept down the hill in their shining car every Sunday morning and went to church.

The minister was grieved, and told Mrs. MacGregor so one day. "How can you love the Lord and treat these people so miserably?" He pointed to the valley. "They are poorly dressed. They do not have proper food. They work hard for you. Can't you see that anything you do for them in Christ's name is as if you do it for Him?"

Treasure Hunt: Matthew 25:34-40

Let's talk about *works*: Our salvation is a gift from God. Our gratitude for this great gift is expressed in our work for Him.

Do you have more than you need while someone you know is in need?

A prayer: Father, forgive my selfishness. Forgive me when I fail to share. Forgive me that I so often put myself first. You didn't, Lord. You always thought of others. Help me follow Your Son's example. Amen.

A song to sing: "Let the Lower Lights Be Burning"

Swelling or Growing?

"May I never boast except in the cross of our Lord Jesus Christ" (Galatians 6:14) ·

"I get awfully tired of hearing Tom brag," Herb told his dad. "He's the fastest runner, the best pitcher, makes the most A's, always has the best of everything—anyway, to hear *him* tell it!"

"Sounds like he's doing more swelling than growing!" Herb's dad grinned.

"What do you mean, Dad?"

"When I was a boy, my folks had a cottage near the seashore. I used to catch a fish that puffed up like a balloon when we hauled it into the boat. It didn't actually grow—it just swelled! That's pretty much what a fellow does when he thinks so much of himself. He gets puffed up, but actually he's smaller than

9

ever, because real worthwhile growth begins in a person's life and comes with the help of God."

"Yeah, Dad, I guess you're right. We don't really have much to be puffed up about, do we?"

"No, Son. All we have comes from God. We can do nothing worthwhile except as Christ works through us."

Treasure Hunt: John 19:25-37

Let's think about this: Whenever we see a cross, it usually occupies a high spot. It rises atop a hill or a church. This is fitting, because the cross is the very peak of all the wonderful things Christ has done for us.

10

A prayer: Dear Lord, never let me forget the cross of Calvary. I am glad some of Your friends stayed by You there under the cross. Always keep me near the cross in my thoughts and actions. I never want to forsake You or take sides against You by wrong-doing. Keep me humble. As the song says, may the cross "be my glory ever." Amen.

A song to sing: "Near the Cross"

A Wonderful Secret!

"Do not let your hearts be troubled. Trust in God; trust also in me" (John 14:1).

"I can't understand how Aunt Lu keeps so cheer-ful," Cindy said. "Uncle Ben has a broken leg, and that makes so much more work for her. She cares for him and has to do all the chores. Last week hail flat-tened her nice garden, yet today when I was there she was smiling as cheerfully as ever. When she was out in the kitchen getting dinner, I heard her singing 'Let not your heart be troubled.' I should think, with all her troubles, she would be sad instead of glad!"

"I know my sister pretty well," Cindy's dad smiled. "Aunt Lu has discovered a wonderful secret."

"What secret?" asked Cindy.

"God reveals many wonderful hidden and secret things to those who live close to Him and trust Him,"

11

Cindy's dad said thoughtfully. "Aunt Lu knows, for she has proved it, that God is greater than any troubles."

Treasure Hunt: Matthew 6:25-34

Let's think about this: What troubles you? If you obey God's commandments, He is ready to help you and give you joy right in the midst of trouble.

A prayer: Dear Lord, thank You for being ready and willing to help me and bless me. Help me to obey. Give me courage to do Your bidding. Keep reminding me it is dangerous to disobey Your commands. Help me bring cheer to those who are discouraged and troubled. In Jesus' name, amen.

A song to sing: "Glory to His Name"

Idols

"You turned to God from idols to serve the living and true God" (1 Thessalonians 1:9).

Don turned around in his Sunday-school chair. He was embarrassed. It was almost his turn to say the memory verse, but he couldn't remember it. He had not finished his workbook assignment, either. He could tell by his teacher's face that she felt sad about it.

When they went into the lesson period, Don became very interested. He was glad he didn't worship idols, like the people in the Bible lesson did! Then his teacher's words brought him up on the edge of his chair.

"I wonder what idols some of you boys and girls worship," she said. "Keep track of your time this week and see."

Don was surprised at the end of the week. He could hardly believe his own record. He found that television was the idol that kept him from reading his Bible, learning Bible verses, doing his workbook lesson, and prayer. He slid through home duties and schoolwork as fast as he could to get to his favorite TV shows. Practically all his spare time was spent in front of the set!

Don decided right then to change, and serve the true and living God!

Treasure Hunt: 2 Kings 17:35-39

Let's think about *idols*: (An idol is anything we think is more important than God.) Can you think of some things that might become idols to us? Find Samuel's recipe to do away with idols in 1 Samuel 7:3. Read it prayerfully.

A prayer: Dear Lord, if there is anything in my heart that should not be there, take it away, please. I do not want to worship anything more than You, Lord. Please keep reminding me to listen to my parents, my Sunday-school teacher, my minister, and my youth counselor. Help me realize that they want what's best for me. Amen.

A song to sing: "I'll Be True, Lord Jesus"

"Blessed Are the Merciful"

"Blessed are the merciful, for they will be shown mercy" (Matthew 5:7).

The Cub Scouts were excited. Their knapsacks hung over their shoulders. They were on a nature

14

hike to collect leaves for their scrapbooks. As they neared the Swanson place, they saw Randall on the front porch in his wheelchair.

"Don't even look in!" one of the boys cautioned. "He'll beg us to stay."

"Hi! Hi, kids!" Randall's eager voice hailed them, but the boys raced past.

Douglas thought uneasily about Randall, who could never run or play or know the joy of racing to catch a ball and feeling it smack into his glove. He didn't even have the simple pleasure of walking. "Let's go back and play with Randall awhile, guys," he suggested.

"Aw, Douglas, we don't have time. We have work to do. You go if you want to be loony, but remember the Scoutmaster said the best scrapbook wins some tickets to a baseball game."

Douglas thought about that as he trudged back alone, but when he saw how happy Randall was to see him, he knew he had made the right decision. They played with Randall's games, and the morning passed quickly. When Randall's dad came home, Randall told him Douglas had given up a hike to play with him.

"Is that so?" Randall's dad grinned. "Trees are my hobby. I have one of every kind that will grow in this area. Some are foreign and some are very rare."

He piled the boys into his car and they rode through the shaded drives of Mr. Swanson's private grove.

He gave Douglas a leaf from each tree and helped him to identify them. When Douglas thanked him, he put a hand on his shoulder and said gently: "You are a merciful boy, Douglas."

Douglas felt good as he spread his picnic lunch on the ground for Mr. Swanson and Randall to share. "Help yourselves," he grinned. "Mom packed a big one. There's plenty for all."

Treasure Hunt: 1 John 3:16-18

Let's think about *mercy:* Jesus said, "Blessed [happy] are the merciful." What did He say that the merciful would obtain? (Matthew 5:7)

A prayer: Dear heavenly Father, thank You for Your mercy and loving-kindness. Thank You for feeling sorry for sinners and sending a Savior to this world. Thank You for forgiving my sins. Help me to be as kind and merciful to others as You are loving and merciful to me. In Jesus' name I ask this, amen.

A song to sing: "Jesus, Tender Shepherd, Hear Me"

The B-L-E-L-E

"Come, let us sing for joy to the Lord" (Psalm 95:1).

Little Deanna tossed her blonde curls. Her blue eyes shone with joy. Right at the dinner table, she suddenly began to sing: "The B-L-E-L-E!" When everyone looked surprised, she said, "That's a song!"

"The B-l-e-l-e?" her family puzzled. "What song is that?"

"We sang it in Sunday school today. The B-l-e-l-e," she insisted.

Finally her dad figured it out. "Do you mean B-I-B-L-E?" he asked.

"Yes," beamed Deanna, "the B-L-E-L-E!"

Though no one figured out at first what song Deanna was singing, Jesus knew at once she was singing praises to Him, and He was pleased. Jesus loves children very, very much. How wonderfully glad He must be when He looks down from Heaven into Sunday schools and hears the voices of children all over the world singing glad praises to Him!

If we think of the words as we sing them, our worship in praise becomes rich and joyful. Paying attention to the words helps us memorize them. Then their message stays in our hearts and minds to make all our lives more joyful!

Treasure Hunt: Psalm 95:1-7

Let's think about *praise:* How many songs and choruses do you know? Have you noticed how hymns tell us what God has done for us and thank Him for His great love?

Singing is a wonderful way to praise God, not only on Sunday but all through the week.

A prayer: Dear Father in Heaven, I am grateful today for the joy in my heart. I am happy I can sing praises to your holy name. I am glad Heaven will be a happy place ringing with joy and music and praise. Thank you for music. Thank you for people who write songs with good words and beautiful melodies. Amen.

A song to sing: "The B-I-B-L-E"

Follow the Trail

"He was despised and rejected by men, a man of sorrows, and familiar with suffering" (Isaiah 53:3).

Winnie had no parents. She was shoved from one foster home to another. Sometimes she was mistreated. She was told so often she was ugly that she became shy and ill at ease. It became hard for her to become friendly or make friends.

But one day someone gave Winnie a new Bible.

Winnie had so few new things! She treasured her Bible and began reading it. In it she found Someone before her who had been "despised and rejected by men, a man of sorrows, and familiar with suffering."

Jesus knows exactly how I feel, she thought. This helped her feel better. Winnie was never as sad or lonely again. She lived by the Book she was reading. She spent her time doing kind things for others. She began to make friends. She was even able to be kind to those who remained unkind to her.

Sometimes we, too, might be rejected and disliked. People might be unkind to us because we will not go along with wrongdoing. They might make fun of us or think we are foolish because of our faith in Jesus Christ. Jesus knows about our feelings and trials, and He will comfort us. The important thing is always to follow the trail He has blazed for us.

Treasure Hunt: Isaiah 53:1-6

Let's think about *troubles:* Life is not all smiles and pleasures. Just as the weather brings both sunshine and rainfall, life has its ups and downs. Sometimes we are misunderstood, sick, or lonely. Whatever our difficulty, Jesus was misunderstood more than we ever will be. He suffered more. He understands and cares when we feel bad.

A prayer: Dear Lord Jesus, thank You for caring. Thank You for strength when I am weak. May my troubles not make me bitter and complaining, but help me grow strong. Amen.

A song to sing: "Jesus Loves Me"

God Is Mighty

"When I am afraid, I will trust in you" (Psalm 56:3).

Wendy's eight-year-old brother Ricky was afraid of the water. Whenever the water came up to his chin he became so frightened he forgot to move his arms or legs.

"You've just got to learn to swim," said Wendy. "We live so close to the lake, it's not safe not to know how. I know why you get so scared. It's because you fell off the pier when you were little. Let's go talk to Dad. Maybe he can think of something that will help you feel safe in the water."

Their dad looked thoughtful. "I'll come out and sit on the pier and hold out a long pole to you, Ricky. You can hold on to it and tread water for a while."

Soon Ricky felt brave enough to let go of the pole as his father sat nearby. Then his father jumped into the water and gave him a swimming lesson.

The psalmist said: "When I am afraid, I will trust in you." God is a loving heavenly Father. He is always close beside you. Ask His help the next time you are frightened or tempted. He will strengthen you.

Treasure Hunt: Psalm 34:1-4

Let's think about this wonderful promise: "The eyes of the Lord are on the righteous and his ears are attentive to their cry" (Psalm 34:15).

A prayer: Lord, help me remember that Your help is

always near. I do not have to depend on my own strength, or do things alone. Thank You for being near. Amen.

A song to sing: "He Is Able to Deliver Thee"

God Has a Plan for Me

"I was not disobedient to the vision from heaven" (Acts 26:19).

"I want to be a missionary to Taiwan some day," said Joan. "Wouldn't you like to be a missionary, too?"

"No," said her brother Jack, "I want to be a football coach."

"But Jack, being a missionary means serving God so much better. We are supposed to tell the gospel to everyone in the world."

"I'm going to be a football coach. That's what I've always wanted to be," insisted Jack. "I can witness to my team."

"Well, I think you're wrong—" Joan began. Their older sister Sandra interrupted.

"Joan," she said, "there are other ways to witness about Christ besides being a missionary or a minister. If God calls you to be a missionary, that's His plan for you. If God calls Jack to be a coach, well, he would be in a very good spot to witness to young fellows about the Lord. God needs workers all over the world in all different kinds of jobs. Just be sure you are obedient when He calls—that's the important thing."

Treasure Hunt: Acts 26:19-23

Let's think about *God's plan for me:* What are your favorite subjects at school? Hobbies? Talents? The things you do best? Think seriously of those things in your life that can be developed and used to bring honor in service to the Lord.

A prayer: "Speak, Lord, for your servant is listening." That was Samuel's prayer. I want to make it my prayer, too. Lord, help me do my best in school. May your Holy Spirit direct me as I study the Bible. "Take my life and let it be consecrated, Lord, to thee." Amen.

A song to sing: "Take My Life and Let It Be"

Marcia's Choice

"I will instruct you and teach you in the way you should go; I will counsel you and watch over you" (Psalm 32:8).

Marcia pushed the big glass revolving door and whirled into the busy department store. "I can hardly wait to pick out my coat," she said, as she and her mother got on the escalator.

The clerk brought out light coats and dark coats; coats with fur and untrimmed coats. Marcia and her mother finally narrowed the choice down to a light colored coat with a tiny fur collar and a gray tweed with tiny blue and red flecks in it.

Marcia stroked the soft fur on the light tan coat. "This one is adorable. Mom, please let me have this one."

A little frown furrowed her mother's forehead. "Try the tweed again, Marcia."

With a sigh, Marcia slipped on the tweed. It *was* nice, too.

"I like that one best," her mother decided. "It's

good for a school coat, yet nice enough for dress. The light coat will soil easily, and it won't wear as well. Soon it will look shabby."

Marcia could not imagine the soft, beautiful coat ever looking shabby. "I want this one!" she said stubbornly. "If I can't have this one, I don't want either one."

Marcia got the coat she wanted. The first time she wore it she got a big smudge on it, and it had to go to the cleaners. She had to be so careful to keep it looking decent that she could not play as she wanted to. The coat soon looked shabby in spite of her care. It cost too much to give away. After a few weeks, Marcia hated the coat every time she put it on.

Treasure Hunt: 1 Samuel 8:4-10, 19-22

Let's think about *demands:* Did you ever demand some gift or favor until someone gave in, and it was yours? Sometimes we just don't know what is best for us. That is why it's important to pray, "If it is Your will . . ."

A prayer: Dear Lord, forgive my stubborness. Sometimes I ask for things that aren't good for me. I thank You that You are wiser than I am, and do not always give me my way. Your way is best. I thank You, too, for parents and leaders who don't always give me my way. Help me to realize, when I'm disappointed, that it is for my good. In Jesus' name I pray, Amen.

A song to sing: "Have Thine Own Way, Lord"

"To God Be the Glory"

"Let him who boasts boast in the Lord" (1 Corinthians 1:31).

Dennis sang a solo at the morning worship service. The people listened as his voice rang out in the beautiful strains of "Jesus, the Stranger of Galilee."

"I enjoyed your song," many of them said. They thanked him for singing.

"I love to sing," Dennis told his mother later, "and I know God gave me my voice. That's why I want to use it for Him."

In the ninth Psalm, David said, "I will sing praise to your name, O Most High." One of the most wonderful ways to praise the Lord is by singing hymns.

When you open the hymnbook, do you *think* of the words, or do only your lips move and sounds come out?

Our hymns have interesting stories behind them. Isaac Watts started when he was young, writing songs to God's glory way back in the eighteenth century. Many of his hymns are in today's hymnbooks.

Treasure Hunt: Psalm 9:1, 2

Let's think about *singing*: How many hymns do you know by heart? What is the author's name? The music composer's name? The writer of the words has his name listed on the left hand side; the music composer on the right.

Can you find a hymn by Isaac Watts in your hymnbook?

Will you now prayerfully decide to do as Dennis did—give your talents to God?

A prayer: Thank You, Father, for music and all its beauty. Thank You that I can make a joyful noise of praise to You with music. Thank You for those who have the gift to write music and words. Bless all who sing and play and use their gifts to Your honor and glory. Use me for Your honor and glory, too, I pray. In Jesus' name, amen.

A song to sing: "To God Be the Glory"

Heave-ho!

"Better to be lowly in spirit and among the oppressed than to share plunder with the proud" (Proverbs 16:19).

"Heave-ho!" the corporal barked orders at the soldiers building the fort. It was a hard job, but the corporal did not offer to help them.

A man on horseback came riding up. He jumped off his horse and helped the soldiers. Then he turned to the corporal and asked, "Why didn't you help them?"

"Me?" the man drew himself up proudly. "Me, help them? Why, I'm the corporal."

The man swung up on his horse. He leaned over and said to the corporal, "The next time you need

26

help with any work you are too proud to do, call George Washington."

How do you suppose that corporal felt as he watched the Commander-in-Chief of all the soldiers in the army ride away?

Treasure Hunt: Numbers 12:3-8

Let's think about *meekness:* What does this word mean to you? Wishy-washy? No backbone?

Study the life of Moses and learn about all the hard things he did. You will find out he was neither wishy-washy nor a man without a backbone. But the Bible says about him, "Now the man Moses was very meek, above all the men which were upon the face of the earth" (Numbers 12:3, KJV).

A prayer: Dear God, help me not to be conceited or proud. I have nothing to boast about. All I have, or am, or hope to be, is because of blessings You've given me. I want to be humble and ready to work wherever I'm needed. Amen.

A song to sing: "I Surrender All"

Van's Lesson

"He who conceals his sins does not prosper" (Proverbs 28:13).

"It seemed like fun," Peter said, "but I don't feel so good now. I think I'll go back and confess."

"Don't go soft!" retorted Van. "And don't you tell on me."

But Peter went back to Mr. Nelson's place. He felt scared, but he told Mr. Nelson that he had been using the red tomatoes in Mr. Nelson's garden for targets when he threw his darts.

"I saw you and Van from the barn window," said Mr. Nelson gruffly. "You can work it off in the garden for me this summer if you want to, but I'm going to make Van's parents pay for the damage he did."

Peter worked many long, hot hours that summer. His dad was proud of the way Peter tried to right a wrong, so he made a down payment on a bike for Peter. Peter finished paying for it at the end of the summer with his paper route money.

When he rode by to show his new bike to Van, Van said sadly, "It'll be a long time before I get a new bike. Dad promised to help me buy one, too, but he had to give that money to Mr. Nelson to pay for the damage I did to his garden."

Treasure Hunt: Hebrews 12:10, 11

Let's think this over: The Bible tells us that "the eyes of the Lord are everywhere, keeping watch on the wicked and the good" (Proverbs 15:3). We cannot hide from God, but when we are sorry for our wrongdoing, we can be glad God is merciful and forgives us freely.

A prayer: Dear Father, I see it is all wrong, according to Your Word, to sin and try to cover it up. Give me courage, Lord, when I do wrong, to confess it to You and make it right with anyone I have wronged. Amen.

A song to sing: "The Heavenly Voice" ("List to the Gospel Resounding")

Cynthia's Mistake

"Everyone who sins is a slave to sin" (John 8:34).

Cynthia thought Ann was the most interesting girl she had ever met when she first moved to town. Ann did many things that were forbidden to Cynthia. *If I could be Ann's best friend,* Cynthia thought, *I'd be the happiest girl in the world!*

Ann began inviting Cynthia to do things and go places with her. Cynthia spent these times with Ann even though she knew her mother would not approve. She started talking like Ann did. She borrowed books and magazines from Ann and hid them in her room. More and more, she found herself doing and saying things Ann did. Sometimes this bothered her.

One day her mother found the hidden books. Then Cynthia confessed: "I thought being Ann's friend would make me happy, but I'm miserable oftener than I'm happy. I do things I know I shouldn't and I can't seem to help it. I just get in deeper and deeper."

" 'Everyone who sins is a slave to sin,' " quoted her mother.

"What does that mean?" asked Cynthia.

"It means sin is the master. The person who sins is like a slave obeying its commands."

Cynthia thought it over. "Yes! That's the way it is!" she exclaimed. "I'm not going to be a slave any longer. I want to be free!"

Treasure Hunt: John 8:34-36; Romans 8:5, 6

Let's think about *slavery:* That's not a pleasant thought, is it? Habits grow stronger the more you use them, so it's important to choose good ones. This Bible verse will help: "Avoid every kind of evil."

A prayer: Father, help me not to become a slave to sin. I want to be free. Help me trust in Jesus, who

30

frees from sin. Take away from my heart the desire to do wrong. Help me choose friends who keep me close to You instead of leading away from You, Father. In Jesus' name, I pray. Amen.

A song to sing: "Just When I Need Him Most"

Doing Our Part

"Do not neglect your gift . . ." (1 Timothy 4:14).

"What's wrong, Jim? You look glum," his mother said.

Jim answered, "Mom, you said if we ask God to help us, He will."

"Yes, He will."

"But, Mom, we had a science test today. I prayed for a good grade last night, and I prayed before the test, but I only got a C-minus."

"Let's see," his mother said. "You came home from school last night and told me you were having a hard test today. Instead of studying, you played ball until dark. Then you and your brother played inside until bedtime. I didn't see you open your science book at all. Did you?"

"No," Jim confessed.

"Well," his mother asked him, "could you honestly expect God to do your work while you were having fun?"

Jim's face wore a shame-faced grin. "No, Mom, of

course not! I had no business to ask God to help me when I hadn't even studied. I should have done my part. Then He could have done His for me!"

Treasure Hunt: 1 Timothy 4:12-16

Let's think about *advantages:* Am I doing my best with all the advantages God has provided me with?

A prayer: Father, thank You for this wonderful world You've given us, and for books and teachers who teach me about it. Thank You for hours of play, too. When I have to choose between study and play, help me make a wise choice, dear Lord. Amen.

A song to sing: "A Charge to Keep I Have"

Where God Looks

"The Lord does not look at the things man looks at. Man looks at the outward appearance, but the Lord looks at the heart" (1 Samuel 16:7).

Kenny was excited. At last he was going to have a pony of his own! He had studied the pictures the owner had sent. One pony was coal black. The other was brown with a white star on the forehead. Kenny had decided the black one was the better looking. He asked his dad to buy him the black pony, but his dad said they would decide when they got there.

As the owner led them out, Kenny saw that the black was a beauty all right. Her sleek coat shone in the sun, but he noticed something the pictures had failed to show. The pony kept stamping her feet, throwing her head about, and flashing her eyes whenever anyone came near her.

The little brown pony nuzzled against Kenny as he patted her soft nose.

"Now which one do you want?" Kenny's dad asked.

"When I came I thought sure I'd pick the black," Kenny said, "but she's so wild. Star is nicer. I want her."

"Oh, so you've already named her?" grinned his dad. "The black pony is a beauty, but I had already made up my mind to buy the brown. She has a kind, gentle disposition."

Treasure Hunt: Psalm 139:1-4

Let's think about *appearances:* Did you ever hear the expression, "Putting your best foot forward"? Some might think this is done by brushing their hair, shining their shoes, and dressing up to impress people. We should be well-groomed both outside and *inside.* God looks within us to see if we are good-looking! What ugly things He sometimes sees inside us!

A prayer: God, forgive me! My heart is often full of sinful thoughts and wrong attitudes. "Wash me and I shall be whiter than snow." In Jesus' precious name I pray. Amen.

A song to sing: "Whiter Than Snow"

A Good Example

"I have set you an example that you should do as I have done for you" (John 13:15).

Jane and Judy shared a bedroom. Jane was thrilled with the bedroom her mother fixed up for them. She kept her things neat. Judy flung her clothes about on chairs or left them in heaps on the floor. Because Jane liked a neat room, she usually ended up, after lots of arguments, cleaning the whole room herself.

On Saturday their parents planned a visit to the city. "You girls may come with us if your room is

clean by the time we are ready to leave," they were promised.

I'll fix Judy, Jane thought grimly. *I'll leave her stuff just like she throws it around.* She picked up and dusted and put her things away. Then she got ready to go to the city.

Judy barged in from play. "Are you ready to go already? Oh, Sis, thanks a lot for cleaning for me again."

"I only cleaned my half," Jane told her. Big tears spilled as Judy said, "Then I can't go, can I?"

Jane couldn't bear to see her sister so unhappy. "I think you can still make it," she said. "I'll help you."

Jane ended up by doing most of the cleaning, but a grateful Judy said, "Thank you, Sis. From now on I'm going to do my best to be a good sister like you."

Treasure Hunt: 1 John 4:9-11

Let's think about *our example:* Jesus came into the world to help others. If we want to be like Him, we will try to be good examples for others, too.

A prayer: Dear Lord, thank You for showing me how to live. Help me to have my eyes wide open and my heart ready to love and help someone today. Amen.

A song to sing: "Oh, How I Love Jesus!"

Rules, Rules, Rules

"The authorities that exist have been established by God" (Romans 13:1).

"I get so sick of rules," said Ivan. "Rules in school, rules at home. Rules! Rules! I'd like to be my own boss."

"Well," said his dad, "can you imagine what a mess there would be without rules? How would you like to play a basketball game without rules?"

"I guess that might not be so good," Ivan said after thinking it over.

"Another thing," his dad went on. "God governs the whole world by rules. He doesn't send us two days in a row or a couple of nights without day. We can count on day following night and on the seasons coming in their order—spring, summer, fall, winter.

"God has put people like your mother and me, your teacher at school, and the policeman on the corner, on this earth to show the ones under our authority how to obey rules and be good citizens. We are responsible to God to do our best, for He is the Supreme Ruler over us all."

"I guess rules are a pretty good thing after all," Ivan said after thinking it over, "and I'm glad I don't have to make them. I'm really not wise enough yet."

Treasure Hunt: Romans 13:1-8

Let's think about *rules:* Authority has its source in God.

Prayer thoughts: Pray for those in authority: Parents, teachers, ministers, the president, the governor, the mayor, policemen. Pray for help in obeying the rules of home, school, country, and God.

A song to sing: "Tell Me the Stories of Jesus"

He Keeps Me
Out of Trouble

"In all your ways acknowledge him, and he will make your paths straight" (Proverbs 3:6).

"Letty," Larry told his twin sister, "the Southside

Boys' Club has asked me to join. I'd be the youngest member of the club. I can't quite figure out why they asked me."

"Are you going to join?" she asked.

Larry answered slowly. "Well, they are a pretty tough gang, but that wouldn't need to make me tough, would it? I just don't know what to do."

"Mom says that when we doubt something, we should trust God and ask His help," Letty reminded.

"I'll do that," said Larry.

The next day Letty dashed into the living room, where Larry was reading a *Sugar Creek Gang* book. She was all out of breath. "I heard something about the Southside boys. I don't think you'd better . . ."

"Oh, that!" Larry looked up from his book and grinned, "I decided to stay out of it."

"Good!" Letty exclaimed. "Ruth Ann just told me her brother joined last year, and they were always in some kind of trouble. Once they were in a bad scrape, they ran off and left Ruth Ann's brother to answer for the whole mess."

"So that's why they want younger boys to join," said Larry. "I'm glad I trusted God to show me the right way."

Treasure Hunt: Psalm 23

What do *you* do when you're in doubt? Sometimes the old saying, "When in doubt, do without" is wise. But prayer is *always* the right thing to do when you're doubtful about what to do, friendships, or other problems.

A prayer: Dear Lord, I trust You to show me the right

way. Following Your path will keep me out of trouble. You are the Light of the World. I want to walk in that light and be a light, too. Amen.

A song to sing: "This Little Light of Mine"

The Greatest Gift

"Unless the Lord builds the house, its builders labor in vain" (Psalm 127:1).

The church was collecting money in a special missionary offering to build a new chapel in Africa.

"I'm going to give a dollar every week this month to the special offering," said Angie, who had lots of spending money.

"I'll give fifty cents," said Ned.

"I only get thirty-five cents allowance, but I'll give twenty-five cents," said Millie.

Everyone else in the class decided to give twenty-five cents a week all that month, except Sue.

"Miss Riley, don't you think we're the most generous class in the whole Sunday school?" asked Beth.

"I can't wait to tell the minister how much good we're doing," said Angie proudly. The rest of the class nodded.

Only two people in the class looked sad—Miss Riley and Sue.

She raised her eyes, and two bright tears quivered there. Everyone in the class knew Sue's father had died recently and that her mother was working to support her family.

"I don't have a dollar or fifty cents or even twenty-five cents a week to give," said Sue. "But I'm going to pray every day that the money the rest of you give will help bring salvation to many boys, girls, men, and women."

Miss Riley's face shone as she hugged Sue happily. "That's what I waited for you all to say. I believe yours is the greatest gift of all. Let's see if our memory verse for today doesn't say so, too."

And all the boys and girls nodded their heads in agreement as they read, "Unless the Lord builds the house, the builders labor in vain."

Treasure Hunt: Mark 12:41-44

Let's think about this: It is the *attitude* with which we give that is important. The Bible tells us that "God loves a cheerful giver." When we cheerfully give Him what we have, He will bless us, whether it is little or much.

A prayer: Dear Father, all I have has come from Your loving hand. Thank You for all my blessings. I want to share my money, my time, and my talents with You. Amen.

A song to sing: "Jesus Saves"

Marching Orders

"I . . . followed the Lord my God wholeheartedly" (Joshua 14:8).

Margie had broken her right arm at the elbow joint. After months of massages and exercises, it was almost well.

"I thought you'd never have much use of your arm again. You had such a bad break," her friend Doug told her.

"I thought so, too, sometimes," Margie nodded, "but Dr. Burnett set it nicely and I know God helped him. When the doctor said, 'Soak your elbow in hot water,' I did. I got very tired of doing it, I can tell you.

41

Many times when I would have rather read or played, I exercised and exercised, even though it hurt."

"It's a good thing you followed orders," said Doug.

"I wanted it to get well right away," Marie said, "but God made bones so it takes them a long time to knit. But the treatment the doctor prescribed helped it heal as soon as possible." She straightened out her arm and bent it back and forth. "I'm glad I followed his orders!" she said happily.

Treasure Hunt: 2 Timothy 2:3, 4

Let's think about *discipline:* Often it seems more pleasant to do as we wish, but discipline plays a big part in making worthwhile people out of us.

A prayer: Father, I want to follow only Christ, because only He is perfect. Help me not to be careless and headstrong, but willing to abide by what is best for me. Keep me faithful and trustworthy through the strength of Jesus, my Lord. Amen.

A song to sing: "Following Jesus"

Count Your Blessings

"Give thanks to the Lord, for he is good. His love endures forever" (Psalm 136:1).

Duane chewed the end of his pencil. How could he

stretch out a Thanksgiving theme to two hundred words? Now if he were Willard, it would be a snap! Willard had everything—good looks, nice disposition, a keen mind, many clothes, the latest sports equipment, a new bike, and a big allowance!

"Count your blessings—name them one by one." That's the way the song went. Well, he had a beat up old bike, not nifty like Willard's, but he was thankful he had it. His ball and glove were old, too. His allowance was slim, but he always had plenty to eat and his clothes were plain but neat. His folks were swell, too—but everything on his list only reminded him of how much Willard had.

The phone rang, and Duane was glad to get away from the theme for a while. It was Willard. "Have you written your theme yet?" he asked. "It should be easy for you. You've got everything a guy could wish for!"

"Everything?" Duane croaked.

"Sure! Swell folks, a home where you can bring friends. I've had some good times there, Duane."

Duane hung up the receiver thoughtfully. Things began to make sense! Willard didn't invite company much, because his folks didn't want the yard and house cluttered up. He couldn't have a dog, either, and his dad was always too busy to do things with him. Willard had said once that his folks didn't believe in God. *I should try to get him to come to church with me,* Duane thought.

Maybe Willard wasn't so lucky after all. Duane's pencil flew down the page. He had wonderful parents, grandparents, uncles, aunts, cousins, friends. He had enough blessings to write twenty themes— wonderful, rich blessings—and back of all of them was God!

43

Treasure Hunt: Psalm 136:1-9

Let's think about our *blessings:* Let's take inventory, and then humbly thank our gracious God for His goodness to us!

A prayer: Dear Heavenly Father, thank You for the blessings of home, parents, and loved ones. Thank You for food and clothes and health. Thank You for church and the Bible. Thank You for Jesus, my Savior. Thank You for Your goodness and all blessings. Help me, Lord, to observe Thanksgiving by thanks-living. Amen.

A song to sing: "Count Your Blessings"

A Boy Helps

"Therefore, as we have opportunity, let us do good to all people, especially to those who belong to the family of believers" (Galatians 6:10).

The story is told of a church in New York called the "Brick Church," because it was the first church in the city of Rochester to be built of bricks.

A congregation of people had a meeting house, but it was not large enough. Meeting after meeting was held to discuss building a new church building, but nothing got done. No one seemed ready to do his part.

One day, early in the spring, the doorbell rang at the minister's home. A little boy stood outside. He had brought a wheelbarrow. In it were two small bricks.

"I brought these bricks to build the new church," the boy said.

The minister was so encouraged that he went out right after breakfast and called all his people, one after another. "The church *is* going to be built," he said. "The first load of bricks is already on the ground!"

When the people heard the story of the little boy's gift, they also became enthusiastic. A large, beautiful church was built after a while, because that little boy honored God and had the faith to give God what he could.

Treasure Hunt: John 6:5-14

Let's think about *sharing what we have:* Sometimes we think, "When I get older, I can serve God better," or "When I have more possessions, I can give more." God wants what we have *now.*

Think about the boy who watched Jesus multiply his lunch to feed thousands. How do you think he felt? Don't you think he was Jesus' follower from that day on?

Prayer thoughts: What do you have that you can share with God? A winning smile? A friendly manner? A beautiful voice? A musical talent? A good mind? A strong body?

Resolve to give Him your all today!

A song to sing: "Mine Eyes Have Seen the Glory"

"Righteousness Exalts a Nation"

"Righteousness exalts a nation, but sin is a disgrace to any people" (Proverbs 14:34).

"Once to every man and nation
Comes the moment to decide;
In the strife of truth with falsehood
For the good or evil side."

These words, written by James Russell Lowell, tell the importance of good citizenship. How we should love our beautiful country, and be thankful that we live in a nation where we may worship God.

A country is just what its people make it! What can we do to help America be the right kind of nation?

Obeying rules and laws are duties of every citizen. Friendliness with our neighbors and compassion for the ill, sorrowful, and friendless are necessary, as well as sharing what we have with them.

Someone once told Abraham Lincoln, "I pray every night that God will be on our side. Do you pray that way, too?"

The wise President answered, "No, I do not pray that way. God is always on the right side. I pray that we will be on God's side."

When we are on God's side, then we are the kind of citizens who help build a righteous nation.

Treasure Hunt: 1 Peter 2:13-17

Let's think about *strength:* If a chain has a weak link, it will break when tested. Lawbreakers are the weak links who undermine the strength and character of their country.

Prayer thoughts: Thank God for America.
Ask His blessing on its leaders and citizens.
Give thanks for laws. Pray for strength to live a good and upright life.

A song to sing: "O Beautiful for Spacious Skies"

"Many a Little Makes a Much"

"Whoever can be trusted with very little can also be trusted with much" (Luke 16:10).

One day Mr. Harms, the owner of the hardware store, asked Sam and Dick to come in after school and help him out. He gave them each a big box of nails of all different sizes. He told them to separate the nails according to size and to put them all in order.

Sam got tired after a little while. "This sure is a boring job," he muttered, looking at the clock every now and then. He began putting some of the little nails in with the bigger ones. He didn't think anyone would notice, and he would finish the job faster that way.

Dick got tired too, but he did the work just as Mr. Harms told him to do. He had not finished his job when the boss came to check, but Sam said, "I'm all done!"

"Finished already?" Mr. Harms looked surprised and pleased all at once. He ran his finger over the nails and discovered what Sam had done. His smile faded.

"Neither one of you knew," he said slowly, "that this job today was just a test to try you out. I wanted to find out who would make the better helper. You see, I have a part-time job open for a boy who does his work faithfully.

"But," he looked straight at Sam, "I have no place here for a boy who will cheat."

Treasure Hunt: Colossians 3:23, 24

Let's think about *faithfulness:* Is anything too small to count?

   The boy or girl who does small duties faithfully often gets chosen for the bigger jobs.

A prayer: Father, help me to remember that You are always watching. There is nothing hidden from You. Help me do each job, large or small, the best I can, for Jesus' sake. Amen.

A song to sing: "I'll Be True, Lord Jesus"

A Two-Way Command

"Do not merely listen to the word, and so deceive yourselves. Do what it says" (James 1:22).

"Mom, we're supposed to make memory verse booklets this quarter, and Amy already has hers done. Does it ever look nice—it even has drawings in color. I wish I could make a nice booklet like that, but I can't draw as well as Amy can. She really worked hard on it. She says it took most of her free time in the evenings for quite a while."

"I'm sure the verses can be a blessing to Amy," answered Bob's mother thoughtfully, "but only as she uses them. Cheer up! I know a very fine 'doer of the Word.' "

Bob looked puzzled. "Who?"

"Remember the boy who shoveled Granny Carson's walks all winter? The same boy dries the dishes for his mother after supper almost every evening. And when his friend Alan broke his leg last summer, who was it that brought him his Sunday-school papers every Sunday?"

"Aw, Mom, that wasn't anything!" said Bob.

"I think it is, and I know the Lord thinks so," his mother added quietly, "because His Word tells us, 'Do not merely listen to the word. . . . Do what it says.' "

Bob's face broke into a big grin. "Does it really say that?"

Treasure Hunt: Matthew 7:24-27

Let's think about *practicing God's Word*: Hearing God's Word is a great privilege, but putting its message into action is greatest of all.

A prayer: Dear Father, I want to be both a hearer and a doer of Your Word. Help me to express Your love to others in the way I live my daily life. In Jesus' name, I pray. Amen.

A song to sing: "Make Me a Channel of Blessing"

Our Best Is Not Good Enough

"He saved us, not because of the righteous things we had done, but because of his mercy" (Titus 3:5).

Gloria was a pleasant, mannerly girl who usually tried to do the right thing, so she felt insulted when someone asked her to become a Christian. "I'm not a sinner," she said. "I don't do bad things. I don't lie, steal, or cheat. I do the best I can."

One day Gloria went boating with some friends. She watched as a fisherman in a nearby boat tried to land a big fish. She stood up, lost her balance, and tumbled overboard. She was terrified until her father jumped into the water and swam toward her.

As she lay resting on the beach, he said, "Do you suppose, Gloria, that I jumped into the water to save you because you dried the dishes for your mother this morning, or because you helped me rake the yard last night, or because you've always tried to be a good girl?"

Gloria laughed. "No, Daddy," she said, "I know it wasn't because of anything I did. It was because you love me."

"That's the way the Lord loves you, only much, much more," her dad said quietly.

Treasure Hunt: Titus 3:4-7

Let's think about *doing our best:* The Bible tells that "all our righteous acts are like filthy rags" compared to the goodness of God.

What does Romans 3:10 and Romans 3:23 tell us?

A prayer: Thank You, dear God, for showing me that I am a sinner and that I need salvation. Thank You for showing so plainly my best won't save me. Thank You for love like Yours. Amen.

A song to sing: "Thank You, Jesus"

An Empty Tomb

"You are looking for Jesus the Nazarene, who was crucified. He has risen! He is not here. See the place where they laid him" (Mark 16:6).

Have you ever visited Lincoln's tomb in Springfield, Illinois, or some other tomb where a famous person is buried?

Perhaps you have heard of the pilgrimages of the Moslems to the city of Mecca, in Arabia. They consider that city holy because it is the birthplace of the prophet Mohammed. In the world today there are almost 600 million Moslems. At least once during his lifetime, if he can, each Moslem must travel to the city of Mecca.

Once a Christian missionary and a Moslem walked together in a garden in Palestine. There they saw the tomb where Christ was probably buried. The Moslem burst out, "We can stand before the tomb of our prophet, Mohammed, but all you have is an empty tomb!"

"Yes!" exclaimed the missionary with great joy. "Praise God this is so! *Our* Savior has risen, as He said. He is a living, loving Savior—our leader and helper day by day."

Treasure Hunt: Mark 16:1-7

Let's think about *victory*: What if Jesus had not risen from the dead? We would have no hope of eternal life!

53

A prayer: Dear God, what a wonderful hope we have because Jesus rose from the dead! Thank You, dear Lord, for Jesus—who not only suffered and died for us, but rose again. Thank You that Jesus is victorious over death. Amen.

A song to sing: "He Lives"

Fervent in Spirit

"Never be lacking in zeal, but keep your spiritual fervor, serving the Lord" (Romans 12:11).

"I feel so thankful, I'm going to try to do something for Jesus every day this week," Bonnie said to Wendy.

"I'm going to study my Sunday-school lesson, learn the memory verse, and be in church next Sunday," said Wendy.

That isn't enough for me, Bonnie thought.

If you had been a private eye following Bonnie that week, you would have discovered several things.

Bonnie helped her mother with the dinner dishes every single night without grumbling. She took care of a little neighbor boy while his mother went to church service, and she didn't accept any money for it because she knew the family was poor. She ran errands for lame Mrs. Watkins. She walked away from a group of friends who were poking fun at the new girl at school.

When the end of the week came, she thought: *I have not done very much for Jesus, but He has made me feel happy. I'll try harder next week.*

Do you think Bonnie was fervent in spirit, serving the Lord?

Treasure Hunt: Romans 12:9-11

Let's think about *being fervent:* Fervor, our dictionary tells us, means intense feeling; warmth. What would you think of a pep club that didn't even bother to cheer the team? Let's get *on the ball* for Christ!

A prayer: Lord, being a Christian is the greatest thing in the world! Help me show my faith with enthusiasm and fervor in warm and loving ways. Help me witness and live faithfully for You. Be with me and help me do this, I pray. Amen.

A song to sing: "Forward"

Strength Through Weakness

"My grace is sufficient for you" (2 Corinthians 12:9).

"I just hate these old glasses!" Coralie threw them

on her bed. "Oh, why do I have to have weak eyes? I've prayed and prayed, but I still can't see my friends across the street without my glasses."

"Our prayers are not always answered the ways we want or think they should be," her mother said. "Even Paul, the great missionary for God, had something that bothered him so much that he called it 'a thorn in the flesh.' He prayed about it three times, but God did not take it away."

"I wonder what it was," Coralie puzzled.

"I don't know, but Paul decided to make the best of it. In his weakness, he relied in God's strength and was content. And do count your blessings, Coralie! You look very nice in your glasses, and you have almost twenty-twenty vision with them, you know."

"Oh, yes! I can see the blades of grass instead of just a green blur. I can read the blackboard from the seat in the back row instead of having to move way up front, and I *am* getting used to them."

"That's my girl," smiled her mother.

"Maybe," Coralie said thoughtfully, "I should thank God *for* my glasses instead of complaining that I have to wear them!"

Treasure Hunt: 2 Corinthians 12:7-10

Let's think about *making the best of our difficulties:* Some things we cannot change. We can't always understand, but one thing we can always do is *trust.* God is always strong, always kind, always near us. The more we trust Him, the stronger Christians we will become!

A prayer: Thank You, Lord, that though I am weak, You are strong. Help me, even through difficulty or pain, to trust that Your way is best. Help me be cheerful and content always, as Paul was. May Your name be glorified by the way I act, I pray. Amen.

A song to sing: "Trust in the Lord"

A Hard Thing To Do

"Love your enemies and pray for those who persecute you" (Matthew 5:44).

Martha bit her lip hard. To be blamed for stealing seemed bad enough, but when it came from her best friend, it was more than Martha could stand. Crystal had turned on Martha when she could not find her scarf. "You're wearing one just like mine, Martha. Are you sure you didn't pick up my scarf?"

How could Crystal accuse her of stealing, especially in front of the whole class? Later when she was alone in her room, Martha tried to pray, but she got nowhere. She had such an ugly feeling in her heart toward Crystal. Finally she prayed: "Lord, help me not to feel this way about Crystal. You know she needs to know You. And help her to find her scarf." Martha felt better after that.

The next day Crystal was absent from school. When the teacher announced a test for the following morning, Martha's first thought was one of gladness. Crystal would probably fail. She always had to study hard for math! But after a while, Martha didn't feel very good inside. She decided to stop in with Crystal's book and tell her about the test.

Crystal looked surprised when she saw Martha. She stammered, "Martha, you're a real friend and I like you, even if you did take my scarf."

Crystal's brother Terry ran in, holding a bit of soaked cloth. "I found your scarf out in the yard. It's soaking wet!"

"Oh, Martha," Crystal said, "I'm always accusing people and losing my temper. Why can't I be like you?"

Treasure Hunt: Genesis 45:1-15

Let's think about this: It's not natural or easy to love

58

those who are unkind to us. It is natural to want to "pay them back." Only the Lord Jesus can help us *want* to return good for evil.

A prayer: Father, sometimes it's very hard to love someone who's been mean to me. But when I think of how much You love me even when I'm bad, I'm grateful for Your kindness. Forgive my sins and help me grow in Christian love. Amen.

A song to sing: "Higher Ground"

God Rewards Faithfulness

"Do not be afraid, Abram. I am your shield, your very great reward" (Genesis 15:1).

"Janet, you have such a fine voice, I think you should use it for the Lord. How about singing in the next youth program?" asked Janet's Sunday-school teacher.

Janet said "Yes," but she wasn't sure.

"I don't know if I can do it, Mom," she said later. "You know how scared I get."

"Talk to the Lord about it," said her mother. "Ask Him to take away your fears, and then trust Him. And practice, Janet, until you can do your part perfectly."

When the time came for Janet to sing, she walked up onto the platform on trembling legs and felt the familiar dryness in her mouth. She took one look at the sea of faces in front of her and gulped a desperate prayer as the accompanist played the opening bars of music. "Lord, I've done my part. Please, Lord, help me."

"Raise your head and sing for Me," Someone seemed to whisper inside. Janet raised her head and opened her mouth. *I must get the message of the song across to the people,* she thought. She was so busy trying to do that, she forgot to be afraid! Later, when many of the people told her what a blessing the song had been to them, she felt humble and thankful inside—and she knew why!

Treasure Hunt: Hebrews 11:8-16

Let's think about *God, our helper:* God made a covenant with Abram. If Abram would keep his part of the bargain, God told him his reward would be very great. God is calling boys and girls today, as He has always done, to separate themselves from wrong things and follow Him.

A prayer: Dear Father, I am thankful that You are so great and good and powerful. Help me to be faithful when I have hard things to do. I'm glad I can come to You for help. I know You will give me strength, because that is one of Your promises. Thank You. Amen.

A song to sing: "Great Is Thy Faithfulness"

Learning From Suffering

"For we do not have a high priest who is unable to sympathize with our weaknesses, but we have one who has been tempted in every way, just as we are—yet was without sin" (Hebrews 4:15).

When Harry fell out of the walnut tree and broke his arm, he wondered why God let that happen to him. Harry liked to play and have fun. He could not do much of that with the big, heavy cast on for six weeks. He was thankful for the friends who stopped by to talk or play games or bring him little gifts.

"If any of my friends ever breaks an arm or a leg or gets sick, I'm going to visit them and try to cheer them up," he said.

When Kendall broke his leg several months later, Harry remembered his own feelings with the broken arm. During the time Kendall had to stay in, Harry stopped by almost every day. Sometimes he helped Kendall with schoolwork. Sometimes he brought Kendall's Sunday-school papers. Other times they played games or enjoyed a book or candy Harry brought along.

Treasure Hunt: Hebrews 4:14-16

Let's think about *God's compassion:* When God became a man, He went through all the hurts and troubles that any person goes through. Because of this, He can understand our problems and needs, and He is able to help us when we need Him.

A prayer: Thank You, dear God, for understanding us and loving us. Thank You for always keeping Your promises to us. Help me to use my hurts to understand others better. Watch over those in pain today. Heal them if this is Your will for them. Amen.

A song to sing: "Sitting at the Feet of Jesus"

Are You Listening?

"He said to them, 'Go into all the world and preach the good news to all creation' " (Mark 16:15).

Amy choked back a lump in her throat. She looked at her Sunday-school teacher sitting way up front in the church in one of the visiting ministers' chairs. Miss Teresa was a very good friend of hers.

Amy thought, *I don't see why she couldn't stay home and teach my Sunday-school class. She can serve God here just as well as across the ocean!*

The preacher began to talk and Amy listened. "God is good to us," he said, "to let us send Miss Teresa to tell people in another land about Jesus. We love her and thank her for what she has done in this church. It's hard to say good-bye, but God has called her to do a bigger work. We must not be selfish."

Amy began to understand. Miss Teresa had to leave. She had often told her Sunday-school class to listen for God's voice and to obey His will. That was what Miss Teresa was doing, Amy realized. She thought, *I will tell her after church how much I love her. I'm going to pray for her every single day, and write to her often.* She clutched her offering money tightly in her fist. *I'm going to give some of my allowance money to missions, too,* she whispered to herself.

Treasure Hunt: 1 Samuel 3:1-10

Let's think about *listening* for God's call: Samuel cheerfully and willingly answered the Lord's calling. He obeyed God, and later he became a leader of all God's people.

A prayer: Dear God, open my ears so I can hear Your voice. Help me to obey it and follow wherever it leads me, all my life. Amen.

A song to sing: "Jesus Is Calling"

He Has Done Great Things

"Go home to your family and tell them how much the Lord has done for you" (Mark 5:19).

Raymond had almost lost his hearing. One day he heard of a doctor who performed ear operations to help people like him. The doctor operated on Raymond's ear. Soon he could hear bird songs, a watch ticking, the soft breezes whispering in the trees—all the sounds he had not heard for a long, long time. The world seemed bright and new and wonderful to him.

Whenever he met anyone who could not hear well, guess what he did? Yes, he told them about his doctor. "You should go to my doctor," he would say. "He helped me. I can hear again."

When Jesus, God's Son, lived on earth, He healed the sick. He made the lame walk, the deaf hear, and the blind see. He fed multitudes of people with a boy's lunch. He even raised people from the dead. His many wonderful works showed His great power and love.

The most wonderful thing Jesus did was to die for sinners. God loves us very much and does great things for us every day. Jesus asked all those who love Him to tell others about Him and about God's great love for them.

Treasure Hunt: John 9:1-11

Let's think about *telling others:* Has the Lord done great things for you? Are you telling others about them?

A prayer: Father, thank You for Your great love for all people. Thank You for sending Jesus to show compassion for the blind, the deaf, the lame, the sick, and the sinful. Thank You for all Your wonderful works. Amen.

A song to sing: "The Great Physician"

Want To Be Great?

"Whoever wants to become great among you must be your servant" (Matthew 20:26).

Would you make your name immortal?
Write it not on earthly things!
Go the way of love and service
As did Christ, the King of kings!
Write it clear in deeds of kindnesses;
Yes, a humble servant be—
For the Lord will then record it
In Life's Book eternally!

Becky is never too busy to help a friend with a problem, help her mother with housework, baby-sit with her brother John, or stay and help her teacher with after-school jobs. Can you guess why Becky is one of the most popular girls in school?

Clarence declined the honor of playing the trumpet solo in the school concert because he could not meet

for practice after school. Later it was found out he had visited lame Tim Prescott every night after school to help him with schoolwork and his Sunday-school workbook. When Tim became a Christian, he said it was because his friend Clarence had shown him the way.

Treasure Hunt: Matthew 20:25-28

Let's think about *greatness:* We are often concerned with our own importance—in what we think, do, and say. We might want to be popular, rich, or well-dressed, thinking that will make us great. But, what did Jesus say one must be to be chief? How did Jesus practice what He preached?

A prayer: Dear Father, help me want to be great only in Your sight, and to be loving and obedient to my parents and teachers. Help me not always to insist on my own way. Amen.

A song to sing: "Thine for Service"

Overcomer

"Blessed are the pure in heart, for they will see God" (Matthew 5:8).

Bob was proud of his new basketball. His little sis-ter Luanne liked to play with it, but she was not strong enough to throw it up into the basket, so she liked to bounce it against the barn wall. Bob told her not to do this, because of the nails sticking out of the old boards.

One day while Bob was away, Luanne took the ball and threw it against the barn wall. A big spike made a hole in the ball. When Bob came back, his basketball was almost flat. Luanne cried when she saw how angry Bob was.

Then Bob thought, *I must forgive my sister, because that is the Christian way.* He asked God to help him. Then he was able to say in a kind voice, "Luanne, Dad will have the ball fixed for me, and I'll be able to play with it after all."

A few days later, Bob brushed against a table and Luanne's best doll crashed to the floor. Bob told her how sorry he was, but she would not forgive him, and she told everyone who would listen about how Bob had broken her best doll.

Bob saved money out of his allowance for a long time. When Luanne's birthday came, he gave her a nicer doll than the one he had broken.

Luanne began to cry. "Oh, Bob, you're so good! I want to be like you!"

Treasure Hunt: Matthew 5:1-12

Let's think about *long-suffering:* Bob did suffer, didn't he? He saw his new basketball damaged. He endured Luanne's tears and unforgiveness, and yet he was able to want to give Luanne a nice gift. It looked as if Bob was a loser all the way, but in the end he won his sister to Christ.

68

A prayer: Dear God, help me to be forgiving and kind. Help me practice what I believe so others will see that I really do follow You and love You. I want to be an overcomer. Amen.

A song to sing: "I Would Be True"

Sammy Stammer

"Be strong and courageous. Do not be terrified; do not be discouraged, for the Lord your God will be with you wherever you go" (Joshua 1:9).

"I have to give a talk in class tomorrow," said Sam. "I get the shivers just thinking about it. Sometimes I stammer when I'm nervous, and the kids are going to laugh if I stammer."

"Here's a Bible verse to help you," said his dad. "Learn it by heart, believe it, and I'm sure it will give you new courage. Even if you do stammer a bit, just hang on to the words of this verse:

" 'Be strong and courageous. Do not be terrified; do not be discouraged, for the Lord your God will be with you wherever you go.' "

Sam prepared his speech carefully and made sure it had some good points in it. He also learned the Bible verse. But when he got up to speak, he saw some of the kids grin at each other. He heard someone whisper, "This will be good—a speech by Sammy Stammer-Box!"

That was all he needed! Sam started his speech: "T-t-t-today—" Then he remembered the Bible verse. He took a deep breath and started again. "Today . . ." he began firmly, and finished his speech without a single stuttering word. He sat down with a big glow of thanks in his heart that the Lord had been with him and given him courage and strength to help him.

Treasure Hunt: Matthew 14:22-33

Let's think about *courage:* As Jesus walked on the water, impetuous Peter flung himself out of the boat, but he sank. He forgot to trust Jesus completely. When we take our eyes off of Jesus, we get into trouble, but when we look to Him for help, He gives all the courage and help we need!

A prayer: Heavenly Father, I want to turn my eyes to Jesus today, knowing He will help me and guide me. Help all the Christians be faithful so that tidings of peace and good will may be spread over all the earth. Help me, Lord, to do my part. Amen.

A song to sing: "Turn Your Eyes Upon Jesus" ("The Heavenly Vision")

Obedience Is Better Than Sacrifice

"To obey is better than sacrifice" (1 Samuel 15:22).

"Tomorrow is Mother's Day," Isabel said to her brother. "I'm going to earn some money and buy Mom a present. Mrs. Wilson needs a baby-sitter."

Bud said, "I think Mom would like help better. You know she's been tired ever since she had the flu."

"I'm tired of doing dishes, cleaning my room, making beds, and working without pay." Isabel tossed her head. "I'm sure Mom would like a pretty gift best. Anyway, I can do my work when I get home from Mrs. Wilson's."

But when she got home she was too tired to do anything but flop into bed. *Am I ever glad I got Mom that elegant bag,* she thought before she fell asleep. *That will show her how much I love her.*

She was awakened next morning by her mother's laugh. She picked up her gift and started for her mother's room, but stopped in surprise at the door. Bud was putting a breakfast tray on his mother's lap.

"Here's my gift, Mom." Isabel came in and handed her the package. Her mother unwrapped it, smiling sweetly.

Bud's smile froze when he saw the bag. "Say— uh—that's swell. Guess you like that, huh, Mom?"

"It's lovely," their mother smiled. "But so is that dusting job you did yesterday after your paper route. And this breakfast—Mmmmm!"

I've never seen Bud look happier, Isabel thought. *My gift is too fancy to be used much. Bud's thoughtfulness is much better. I wish I had listened to Bud and shown my love by helping, too.*

Treasure Hunt: 1 Samuel 15:17-22

Let's think about *willfulness:* King Saul did not follow God's orders, but he thought he could please God anyway by offering a sacrifice to Him. But this is not the way God wants us to be. He would rather have our love and obedience than our gifts.

Prayer thoughts: Ask God to help you honor your parents by obeying them and doing things that will make them happy.

Thank God for your home and parents.

Ask God to help you do your best to make home a happy place.

A song to sing: "Where There's Love at Home"

Why Should I Give Up for Him?

"Keep on loving each other as brothers" (Hebrews 13:1).

Roger felt almost sick. He had practiced until he knew the processional perfectly. Then Miss Gray called him aside and asked if he minded if Eldon would play it.

I'm in Sunday school every Sunday, Roger thought bitterly. I learn the verses, pay attention, and do my lessons. Eldon comes whenever he wants to, or if his folks aren't going someplace. He clowns around and doesn't bother to learn the lesson. Why should I give up anything for him?

But the more he thought, the more it seemed a voice inside insisted. Roger prayed about it, and he finally told Miss Gray it was okay for Eldon to play the processional.

Because of this, Roger began to take a special interest in Eldon, and he helped him until he could play the music well. Eldon came regularly to practice. He became so enthusiastic his parents started coming to church, and eventually they accepted Christ—all because one boy was faithful and loving.

Treasure Hunt: Romans 15:1-6

Let's think about *love:* The Bible tells us that love is kind. Sometimes it means taking second place.

A prayer: Father, teach me how to be kind and courteous to everyone. Help me share some of the good things You have given me with some of those who do not know You as I do. Help me to take second place, if that might help someone else learn to know and serve You, Lord. In Jesus' name I pray. Amen.

A song to sing: "More Love to Thee"

Blessed Are the Peacemakers

"Blessed are the peacemakers, for they will be called sons of God" (Matthew 5:9).

Stanley was busy. His dad had promised him to play ball that afternoon if he cleaned the basement in the morning. But every time Stanley went back for a new load of trash, Alec, a neighbor boy, came and scattered the trash all over the lawn and the street. Each time Stanley had to clean it up.

"I don't see how I'll ever get the job done at this rate," Stanley told his little brother Lonny, who was tagging at his heels.

"Sock him, Stanley, sock him real good! You can beat him up! You're stronger than he is!"

Stanley thought for a moment. "I could beat him up, but I know God wants me to be kind instead." For a long time he had been inviting Alec to the church Trailblazer group. "I think I know a better way," he told Lonny.

Alec turned to run when the boys came out of the basement. "Wait, Alec!" Stanley called. "If you help me clean out this basement, I'll help you deliver your papers this afternoon. Then we'll both be done early enough to play some ball."

Alec looked sheepish as he walked slowly toward Stanley and Lonny. "It's a deal!" he said.

Treasure Hunt: Romans 12:17-21

Let's think about *peacemakers:* The Bible says, "Do not repay anyone evil for evil. . . . Overcome evil with good." This is the way to live at peace with others.

A prayer: Father, help me to worship You as I ought to. You are pure and holy, and I praise You! Help me to have a forgiving heart. Help me understand how people might be helped instead of punished. Amen.

A song to sing: "I Would Be True"

The Web of Sin

"The love of money is a root of all kinds of evil" (1 Timothy 6:10).

Benny worked at Hanson's Food Market after school. He didn't think he was being paid enough. *Some day I'm going to have lots of money and maybe even a big store like this,* he thought.

As he swept one evening, he found a fat billfold full of green bills. Twenty-five dollars! He was rich! He decided not to tell anyone. *I'll buy the things I want a little at a time so no one finds out,* he thought.

He bought a new baseball, a good catcher's mitt, a new stamp album. His mother thought he was spending what he earned instead of putting his money into the bank. Then one Sunday the preacher said, "The love of money is a root of all kinds of evil."

Benny's heart pounded. He felt frightened as he thought, *The preacher must have found out about me!* After that, nothing was fun. He couldn't enjoy working or playing or even eating. He could hardly stand the sight of his new things. Finally his burden of guilt became so heavy that he took the billfold to Mr. Hanson and told him the whole story.

"I'll work three weeks free to make up all I took," he promised.

"The owner of this is going to be mighty happy," said Mr. Hanson. "He's an old man and lives on a tiny pension. I'm certain he has gone hungry and missed many meals since he lost his billfold."

Benny shivered. "I've bought things I had no right to have. I've lied. I've cheated. I've stolen. I've caused an old man hunger and worry. I didn't realize how many sins would come into my life because I loved money so much."

Treasure Hunt: 1 Timothy 6:6-12

Let's think about this: One sin leads to another. Like a spider spinning a web around a fly, so sin encircles and binds us. Bad habits are hard to break.

A prayer: Father, help me to be content with what I have. You have blessed me with so many good things. Thank You for them, Lord. Help me to use those blessings in good ways instead of grumbling and wishing for more. Amen.

A song to sing: "Yield Not to Temptation"

Hide the Word

"I have hidden your word in my heart that I might not sin against you" (Psalm 119:11).

The warning bell rang as Bill slid into his seat. He put his hand into his desk but quickly pulled it out again, with a stiff, funny look on his face. His new yellow plastic pencil box in the shape of a rocket was gone!

He glared at the red braids in front of him. Kathy! He remembered how she had looked at it yesterday. "That's exactly the kind my brother Herman wants," she had said.

Bill put his pencil out to poke Kathy in the back, but then a thought stopped him: "Do not judge, or you too will be judged."

He felt hot and ashamed and mixed up. He couldn't just accuse Kathy without proof. Then Kathy turned around, her brown eyes wide with mischief. "Guess what?" she said, and she held out the pencil box! "You must have been in a big hurry yesterday," she laughed. "Look what I almost stepped on out in the aisle!"

Bill gulped "Thanks" as he took the pencil box, but his real thanks was for the Word of God he had hidden in his heart, which had kept him from sinning.

Treasure Hunt: Psalm 119:9-16

Let's think about *judgment*: Why is it dangerous to jump to conclusions?

78

A prayer: Dear Lord in Heaven, I want to be like David—a person after Your own heart. Help me to store Your Word up in my heart to keep me from sinning. Help me not to judge others by what they do or say, and leave judgment to You, Lord. For only You can look into people's hearts. In Jesus' name I pray, Amen.

A song to sing: "Thy Word Have I Hid in My Heart"

The Place to Start

" 'Not by might nor by power, but by my Spirit,' says the Lord Almighty" (Zechariah 4:6).

Emily slammed down the receiver. "I'm going to give up on Nancy," she said. "Every time something special comes up, she chucks Sunday school overboard. I've asked her to come to Sunday school and church with me all year. I even asked my teacher to let her be class secretary in my place this month. What good does it do?"

"Have you tried praying?" asked her mother.

Emily's eyes widened. "Why, uh—no, not much. That's where I should have started, isn't it?"

The next time Nancy refused to go to Sunday school because of other plans, Emily said, "Well, I'll be praying you'll go next Sunday."

Three months later, Emily asked, "Nancy, you haven't missed Sunday school in months, have you?"

"No," Nancy laughed. "I can't. Whenever I'm tempted, something tells me that you're praying I'll go—and I just can't do anything else but go!"

"Oh, Nancy!" said Emily, and she hugged her friend. "I'm so glad!"

"It's a wonderful feeling to have a friend who prays for you," Nancy said.

Treasure Hunt: Matthew 7:7-11

Let's think about *prayer:* Through prayer, God does things that would perhaps not otherwise be done.

A prayer: Father, I want to pray now for those of my friends who do not know You. Help me do my part in telling them about Your love. In Jesus' name, I pray, Amen.

A song to sing: "I Am Praying For You"

A Wisher or a Doer?

"Sing to the Lord a new song, for he has done marvelous things" (Psalm 98:1).

It was getting close to Christmas, and the Sunshine Class was talking about how to celebrate Christmas so that Jesus would be honored on His birthday.

"I wish I could have lived on earth when Jesus was

born," said Dennis. "Then I could have done something for Him."

Deanna smiled at him from across the table. "You can do things for him now," she said. "Like bringing other kids to Sunday school, obeying your parents, running errands, playing with your little brother, being kind . . ."

Dennis's eyes widened. "You're right! I never thought about it that way. Say—why can't the Sunshine Class bring gifts and sing carols for the families over in the mill district? Those kids aren't going to have much of a Christmas with their dads laid off until the spring rush begins."

"That's a wonderful way to honor Jesus!" said the rest of the class.

After he had seen the joy the Christmas plans had brought, Dennis said, "Well, I know one thing. After this I'm not going to be just a wisher. I'm going to be a doer!"

"Me, too!" said Deanna.

Treasure Hunt: Matthew 2:1-12

Let's think about *gifts:* Do you ever yearn to give the Lord Jesus something for all He has done for you? *Give me Your heart and life,* says the Savior of men.

A prayer: Dear God, thank You for sending Jesus to be the Savior of the world. Thank You for such wonderful love. Help me to do what I can to make this world a better place. I know this is Your will for me. I pray in Jesus' name, amen.

A song to sing: "O Little Town of Bethlehem"

Not a Bit Alike

"Let your light shine before men, that they may see your good deeds and praise your Father in heaven" (Matthew 5:16).

"They're not a bit alike, are they?" Dolly overheard a neighbor talking to her mother. "I have never seen twins so different. Polly is such a wonderful Christian sunbeam!"

Dolly felt indignant. Wasn't she a Christian, too? But the words set her thinking—just how was Polly so different?

She heard the front door open and close; Polly was home. She had stayed after school today, to dust erasers and straighten the room for the vacation Bible school teacher.

Dolly heard baby brother Neddy laugh as Polly started to romp with him. "I carried some groceries for Mrs. Fosson after helping my teacher, Mom," Polly explained. "That's why I'm late."

Dolly thought about how Polly was always carrying packages, running errands, making someone smile, taking care of Neddy. Polly *was* nice. No wonder the neighbor thought of her as a sunbeam—she was always glowing with happiness. She enjoyed telling others about Jesus.

I'm not a shining Christian like Polly, Dolly decided. *I hide my light and Polly shines hers out. From now on, I'm going to try to shine like Polly,* she resolved.

Treasure Hunt: Matthew 5:14-16; Ephesians 5:8-10

Let's think about *shining:* Jesus said that we should let our light shine. How can I let my light shine for Him today?

A prayer: Dear Lord, please keep me shining for you. Help my witness make the world just a bit brighter. You are the light of the world, Lord Jesus. Help me live in that light. Use me to help others. Amen.

A song to sing: "Jesus Bids Us Shine"

Hospitality

"Offer hospitality to one another without grumbling" (1 Peter 4:9).

"Why do we always have to let visiting preachers and missionaries spend the night here?" Ellen grumbled.

"We don't always," her dad smiled, "and you know it!"

"Pretty near," Ellen pouted. It just wasn't fair. She was the one who had to give up her bed and sleep on the davenport. She didn't usually care too much, but this weekend she had planned to ask her friend Lucille over.

The missionary came, and told Ellen's family about boys and girls who roamed the streets and foraged in garbage cans for food. Ellen learned that the missionary preached to many who had never heard about Jesus, God's Son. She saw by the pictures the missionary showed that he, too, lived very simply.

"Let's use our good dishes and silver, and our prettiest linens, every meal," Ellen begged her mother. "And please, Mom, cook some of our special dishes. This missionary deserves the best."

"I'm so ashamed," she said after he had gone. "I won't complain about entertaining again. I wouldn't have missed the missionary's visit for anything."

"Yes," agreed the rest of the family. "He brought us far greater blessings than anything we have been able to do for him."

Treasure Hunt: Luke 10:38-42

Let's think about *Christian hospitality:* If Jesus came to your home, you would welcome Him gladly, wouldn't you? It must please Jesus very much when we show kindness to those who work for Him in full-time service.

A prayer: Dear Lord Jesus, help me to remember to make You welcome in my home. Help me to be kind to my family, to be helpful and obedient, and to make my home a happy place where Your Spirit will feel welcome. Thank You for missionaries who work so faithfully for You. Help me to be a missionary in my own way, wherever I am. Amen.

A song to sing: "Bring Them In"

Count Me In!

"We do not have a high priest who is unable to sympathize with our weaknesses" (Hebrews 4:15).

Chet stopped by to walk with Len to school. *It's fun to be with Chet,* Len thought. *He's so friendly and cheerful.* Chet was popular, too. He had been elected president by the class.

As they walked along, Len saw Pat on his front porch waiting for him as usual. Pat was another story! He was a nuisance—always waiting to be entertained. Pat was crippled. No one took very good care of Pat. He was usually dirty. Sometimes his clothes were smelly.

I'll scrooch down behind the hedge. Maybe he won't see me, Len thought. But Pat yelled, "Hey Len, c'mere!" Len pretended not to hear, but Chet stopped and turned in. Sure enough, Pat came up

with the same old thing. "Len and me, we're best friends!" he told Chet.

"It's good to have friends like Len," Chet said. "I'm your friend, too." He took Pat's chair and turned it so the morning sun wouldn't shine in his eyes.

"Here's a new ball point," he said. "Why don't you draw some pictures today? Len and I will stop by after school and look at them."

"Poor kid!" Chet said as he and Len walked down the street, remembering Pat's delight. "I'm going to help him all I can.

"I was often sick when I was little. I know what it means to have good friends. Let's get our heads together, Len, and help him out."

"Count me in!" Len said humbly.

Treasure Hunt: Mark 6:53-56

Let's think about *compassion*: Think carefully, and do something kind today for someone who needs your compassion.

Prayer thoughts:
Give thanks for compassionate Jesus.
Pray for a tender heart.
Ask for guidance to share kindness.
Ask God to express His love through your life.

A song to sing: "More Love to Thee"

"All Are Precious In His Sight"

"From one man he made every nation of men, that they should inhabit the whole earth" (Acts 17:26).

"Come on, Carol, don't play with *them*." Sheila wrinkled her nose as she spoke of the new boy and girl who had come to their school. "They're DP's, you know. Let them alone."

Carol found out that DP meant "displaced person"—people who had to leave their countries because of war and enemies who have taken their homes and their possessions.

I'm glad they could come to a place like our great country of America, she thought. They looked lonesome and sad, so Carol smiled at them and asked them to come with her and play after school.

"I can't be unkind to them and refuse to play with them," she told Sheila. "God loves people of other nations just as much as He loves Americans—and so should I."

Treasure Hunt: Acts 17:24-28

Let's think about *races:* People may have different color skins, but the Bible tells us that God doesn't play favorites—all people are equally precious in His sight.

   Should we act differently than God toward other races and nationalities than our own?

A prayer: Lord, help me to be kind and courteous and Christian in my actions to all people. Help me remember the chorus I sing sometimes—"Red and yellow, black and white/All are precious in His sight." Amen.

A song to sing: "Jesus Loves the Little Children"

Good Forgetters

"Be imitators of God, therefore, as dearly loved children" (Ephesians 5:1).

Darwin bounded in after school and sniffed hungrily. His mother was busy ladling soup into a jar, and it smelled good.

"Darwin," she said, "please take this soup to Mrs. Godwin. Be careful—it's steaming hot. Don't loiter on the way and it will stay hot and taste good when you get there with it."

"Mom!" exclaimed Darwin. "Have you forgotten how Mrs. Godwin talked to you last week when all we did was ask her to go to church with us? You don't need to send that crabby lady any soup. I don't want to take it to her!"

"If you don't go, Darwin, I'll have to go myself, but I'm busy getting supper and the baby needs to go to bed. Mrs. Godwin is ill, Son. She needs our help and love. She needs God, too, all the more perhaps because she doesn't realize it."

"Okay, Mom, wrap it up. If you can forget the way she treated you, I guess I can take the soup over to her." He grinned as he left the house. "God wants us to be good forgetters, doesn't He?"

Treasure Hunt: Matthew 5:39-48

Let's think about *forgetting:* Often those who need to be loved the most are the hardest to love! Sometimes it's hard to be kind, but Jesus can help us return good for evil.

A prayer: Heavenly Father, You are the best forgetter of all, for Your Word says that if we are sorry for our sins, You will send them away and remember them no more. Thank You for this wonderful promise! Help me to be a good forgetter when I am ill treated. In Jesus' precious name, I pray. Amen.

A song to sing: "I Love to Tell the Story"

Unfailing Love

"Have mercy on me, O God, according to your unfailing love" (Psalm 51:1).

Most of the boys and girls thought Mr. Carewe was the crabbiest man in town. Sometimes he shook his fist at them as they loitered on the sidewalk outside his yard. When he broke his hip, most of the kids decided it was good enough for him.

April thought Mr. Carewe must be the unhappiest man in town. She felt sorry for him. *Maybe,* she thought, *I can cheer him up by sending him a get well card or a box of candy.* She had the feeling that the Lord wanted her to visit him, but she was afraid to go.

Finally she went to her minister and said, "No one visits Mr. Carewe. I feel sorry about that."

"I'm glad to hear your concern," said the minister. "He has never let me into his house. Maybe you can pave the way." He gathered some church literature for April to take to Mr. Carewe. Then the minister prayed for Mr. Carewe. He prayed, too, that God would make April brave enough to visit him.

April's heart pounded against her ribs as the nurse let her in. Mr. Carewe's face looked angrier than ever. His black eyes seemed to pierce through April. "What do you want, girl?" he said in a shrill voice. April mumbled something about being sorry he was hurt and that she had brought him something to read.

She stumbled out, thinking, *I didn't do a bit of good.* But she kept on praying.

Then one day Mr. Carewe sent for the minister. Mr.

Carewe had become a changed man. He would never forget, he said, God's loving kindness and mercy in sending April to visit him.

Treasure Hunt: Acts 4:13-20

Let's think about *love:* Can love be shown in any better way than telling about the love of Christ, and best of all in showing His love in action?
How can we show kindness to others?

A prayer: Heavenly Father, thank You for the wonderful example of Peter and John in speaking boldly for You. Thank You for the Holy Spirit, who gives power and courage to witness. Help me be faithful to tell about Jesus. Amen.

A song to sing: "Holy Spirit, Faithful Guide"

Who Cares About Just One?

"I am the good shepherd. The good shepherd lays down his life for the sheep" (John 10:11).

Have you ever been lost? If you have, you know it is an unpleasant experience.

Little Dennis and his mother visited a big department store. There were many bright displays and interesting things to look at. For a few moments, the mother took her eyes off her son. Suddenly she looked back and saw that Dennis was not by her side. He had walked off to another part of the store.

Do you think that mother was interested then in anything that store had to sell? She forgot everything but the thought of her little boy, and she searched throughout the store until she found him. Then she swept him up in her arms and hugged him. Both Dennis and his mother were very happy they had found each other!

In the Bible story for today, one sheep out of the fold of one hundred is lost. But the shepherd didn't say, "I have ninety-nine others. I don't need to go to all the trouble of searching for just one little lost lamb." He went to find the lost lamb and brought it back to the sheepfold with great rejoicing. This is a picture of our loving shepherd, Jesus.

Did Dennis's mother say, "Oh well, just one little boy is lost"? Of course not! She looked until she found him. Does Jesus care if you or I are lost from

Him? Yes! He loves us and cares so much that He died for us.

Who cares about "just one?" Jesus! That's who!

Treasure Hunt: Luke 15:3-7

Let's think about *God's care:* Does this Scripture passage make you feel you are important to God? You are very precious to Him!

A prayer: Thank You, God, for telling me in the Bible how much You love me. Thank You that I don't have to be lost from You, but I can be part of Your flock, and You will be my shepherd forever! Amen.

A song to sing: "Jesus Loves Even Me"

Weak Spot

"Let us throw off everything that hinders and the sin that so easily entangles, and let us run with perseverance the race marked out for us" (Hebrews 12:1).

Paul and his dad were building a fence. As Paul pounded in a nail, his dad warned, "Careful! The nail is going in crooked."

Paul yanked it sideways and it came out crooked. He stared at it, then said, "Oh well, I'll pound it out nice and straight again."

But Paul's dad shook his head. "It might look almost straight, but it will be weakened and bend again, the same place where it bent the first time."

"Let me try to straighten it out, Dad," said Paul.

"Go ahead," said his dad.

Paul hammered the nail carefully. "It looks pretty good now, Dad. I'll pound it into the fence post nice and straight." But even though he hit the nail carefully, it began to bend.

"You were right, Dad," Paul said.

"There's a lesson here for you and me, Paul," said his dad. When we yield to temptations, we're like that nail. We have a weak spot. When Satan finds that he can dent our Christian armor, then that's the spot he attacks again. Sin leaves its marks on us."

"I see what you mean," Paul nodded. "It's better never to start bad habits that make us weak and all bent out of shape. Then we'll never have to work hard to get rid of them."

Treasure Hunt: Hebrews 12:1, 2

Let's think about *bad habits*: You are living in the habit-forming days of your life. Carrying a lot of bad habits around with you can make it very hard to live for Jesus.

Prayer thoughts: Ask God for the strength to form good habits of service, clean speech, daily Bible reading, prayer, and attendance at Sunday school and church.

Pray that you wil form habits that will give you a happy, useful life.

A song to sing: "Yield Not to Temptation"

The Most Important Search

"They received the message with great eagerness and examined the Scriptures every day" (Acts 17:11).

Joe, his mother, father, and sister Suzanne were on vacation in the mountains. They climbed some of the trails and gathered wild flowers of mountain laurel and scarlet paintbrush. They smelled the crisp, delightful air and watched the mountain deer as they walked along.

"Dad," puzzled Suzanne the evening before they left for home, "how did you know the way to get to the mountains? You decided in the morning where we were going, and at night we got here!"

"Dad studied the map that told him how to get here," Joe told her. "Haven't you seen us looking at it as we rode along?"

"I want to look at the map," said Suzanne.

"Boy!" Joe said blissfully as he spread it out before her, "this has been one great trip! That road map sure led us to some beautiful places, nice people, and good places to eat. It kept us from getting lost, too. Maps are important, aren't they, Dad?"

"Yes, they are," said their father.

"And that old map is going to lead us home tomorrow," said their mother.

"Speaking of maps," said their dad, "there is another map I hope you both study all your lives."

"Do you mean the Bible?" asked Joe.

"Yes," smiled his father. "That's where God speaks and tells us the directions for life's journey!"

Treasure Hunt: Isaiah 55:6-11

Let's think about _searching:_ Treasure hunts are fun! I hope you are discovering that in the Bible, you can find the biggest treasures of all.

A prayer: Thank You, dear Lord, for Your Word, the Bible. Help me understand it as I read it. May Your Holy Spirit guide me and bless me every day as I hunt for Bible treasures. Help me store its directions in my heart, to believe and follow You all the days of my life. In Jesus' name, amen.

A song to sing: "Wonderful Words of Life"